The Tomb

A Haunting Lovecraftian Tale of Madness and Supernatural Terror

A Modern Translation

Adapted for the Contemporary Reader

H.P. Lovecraft

Translated by Tim Zengerink

Table of Contents

Preface - Message to the Reader

What If You Could Help Rebuild the Greatest Library in Human History?

Thousands of years ago, the Library of Alexandria stood as the crown jewel of human achievement — a sanctuary where the collected wisdom of every known civilization was gathered, preserved, and shared freely.

And then, it was lost.

Through fire, conquest, and the slow erosion of time, humanity lost not just books — but ideas, dreams, discoveries, and stories that could have changed the world forever.

Today, the Library of Alexandria lives again — and you are invited to be a part of its restoration.

Our mission is simple yet profound:

To rebuild the greatest library the world has ever known, and to translate all timeless works into every language and dialect, so that no seeker of knowledge is ever left behind again.

By joining our movement to rebuild the modern Library of Alexandria, you become part of an unprecedented mission:

- **Unlimited Access to the Greatest Audiobooks & eBooks Ever Written:**

  Instantly explore thousands of legendary works—Plato, Shakespeare, Jane Austen, Leo Tolstoy, and countless more. All instantly available to read or listen, placing a complete literary universe at your fingertips.

- **Beautiful Paperback & Deluxe Editions at Printing Cost**

  Own any title as an elegant paperback, deluxe hardcover, or stunning collectible boxset—offered to you at true printing cost, delivered straight to your door. Build your personal Library of Alexandria, crafted for beauty, built for durability, and worthy of proud display.

- **Fresh Translations for Modern Readers—in Every Language & Dialect**

  Enjoy timeless masterpieces reimagined in clear, contemporary language—no more outdated phrases or obscure references. Alongside the original versions, we're tirelessly translating these classics into every language and dialect imaginable, ensuring accessibility and understanding across cultures and generations.

- **Join a Global Renaissance of Literature & Knowledge**

  You directly support expanding our library, publishing deluxe editions at true cost, translating works into all global languages, and bringing humanity's greatest stories to people everywhere. By joining today, you're not just preserving a legacy of masterpieces; you set in motion a powerful wave of literary accessibility.

Become a Torchbearer of Knowledge.

Join us for free now at **LibraryofAlexandria.com**

Together, we will ensure that the light of human wisdom never fades again.

With gratitude and a shared love of knowledge,

The Modern Library of Alexandria Team

Visit:

www.libraryofalexandria.com

Or scan the code below:

Introduction

Buried Memories: Madness, Ancestry, and the Allure of the Grave

"The Tomb," written in 1917 and first published in 1922 in The Vagrant, stands among H.P. Lovecraft's earliest forays into the eerie world of inherited horror, ancestral identity, and psychological disintegration. Though relatively short and often overshadowed by his more expansive mythos stories, "The Tomb" is a foundational piece in Lovecraft's development. It presents a microcosm of the thematic obsessions that would later define his cosmic horror—lineage, destiny, forbidden knowledge, the pull of antiquity, and the fragility of the mind when confronted with truths that do not align with reality.

The story unfolds as a first-person confession from Jervas Dudley, an aristocratic recluse who recounts his strange obsession with the tomb of the long-dead Hyde family, located near his family's estate. From childhood, Jervas feels drawn to the crypt, experiencing dreams, visions, and sensations that suggest a past he never lived—or perhaps lived long ago. He begins to identify with the deceased members of the Hyde family, especially one in particular, and through a mix of dreamlike exploration and sleepwalking, he descends into a fugue state in which his present identity dissolves into something ancient and spectral. Ultimately, the reader must determine whether Jervas is mad—or if his ancestral blood has awakened something far more terrifying.

This ambiguity—between insanity and supernatural inheritance—is central to "The Tomb." Lovecraft's narrator blurs the boundary between delusion and revelation, madness and memory, fantasy and fact. What begins as a gothic tale of curiosity soon becomes a study in the eerie synchronicities between past and present, the buried and the conscious. And unlike Lovecraft's later tales, where the horror often lies in the vastness of the cosmos, here the horror lies within. It is in the mind, the bloodline, the ancient architecture of family history.

This psychological dimension makes "The Tomb" unique among Lovecraft's works. While it still features his characteristic florid prose, love of antiquarianism, and fixation on decay, it is more introspective, more dreamlike, and more intimate than his larger mythos narratives. It reads like a descent into memory—not the memory of an individual, but of a bloodline. A memory stored not in the brain, but in the bones.

Gothic Revival and the Descent into Identity

"The Tomb" is Lovecraft's homage to the gothic tradition. Readers familiar with Edgar Allan Poe will immediately detect the influence of works like "The Fall of the House of Usher" and "Berenice," where aristocratic decay, morbid obsession, and crumbling estates reflect inner psychological ruin. Jervas Dudley is a quintessential gothic protagonist: pale, bookish, mentally fragile, and obsessively drawn to places that embody his inner condition. The Hyde tomb, sealed and overgrown, becomes a metaphor for the dormant aspects of his personality—his desire to escape the banalities of modern life, his identification with the past, and his yearning to become someone other than himself.

But Lovecraft does more than imitate Poe—he expands on him. Where Poe's stories focus on mental illness and neurosis, Lovecraft hints at something more metaphysical. Jervas's dreams, his ancestral knowledge, and his growing dissociation from the present world suggest not just psychological collapse but spiritual possession. He is not merely a madman—he may be a reincarnated soul. Or a vessel for ancestral memory. Or a man whose lineage is so powerful it reshapes his consciousness.

This layering of horror—personal, ancestral, and spectral—gives "The Tomb" a peculiar power. The tomb itself is not haunted in the conventional sense. There is no explicit ghost, no supernatural event witnessed by multiple characters. Instead, the haunting is internal. The horror is that Jervas cannot distinguish between dream and waking life, between memory and imagination. And Lovecraft, masterfully, refuses to resolve this ambiguity. He offers evidence both for madness and for supernatural continuity, and leaves the reader in the same liminal space as the narrator.

Thematically, this tale introduces what would become one of Lovecraft's recurring ideas: that modern man is not free, but bound—by blood, by history, by knowledge. Jervas is not merely curious about the past; he is claimed by it. The tomb does not invite him—it summons him. And his descent is not a mistake, but a fulfillment. He becomes who he was always meant to be. In this sense, "The Tomb" is Lovecraft's early meditation on predestination and the collapse of identity under the weight of the ancestral.

It is no coincidence that Jervas is dismissed as mad by the outside world. Lovecraft often framed his narrators as unreliable, not because they lied, but because they had seen too much. Madness, in Lovecraft's fiction, is the natural consequence of enlightenment. It is what happens when the human mind touches something it was not designed to grasp. In "The Tomb," this "something" is not alien or cosmic, but familial. It is blood memory. And it is just as overwhelming.

Influence, Reinterpretation, and the Modern Reader

While "The Tomb" is often read as an early, somewhat derivative piece of gothic fiction, it is far more than an apprentice work. It anticipates many of Lovecraft's most enduring themes and offers a clear glimpse into the mind of a writer already obsessed with ancestry, memory, and the blurred boundaries of consciousness. It also contains some of Lovecraft's most accessible prose. Though still rich with archaisms and classical references, the narrative is more focused and intimate than his later mythos epics.

The tale's influence can be seen in numerous psychological and horror works that explore ancestral inheritance and the call of the past. Films like The Others, Hereditary, and Crimson Peak echo the themes of The Tomb—in which family history is both a mystery and a curse. The concept of ancestral guilt, inescapable fate, and the pull of forbidden places continues to animate horror fiction today, and Lovecraft's early experiments with these ideas paved the way for such narratives to flourish in modern form.

Moreover, "The Tomb" speaks to the alienation of the individual in a world that demands conformity. Jervas is not merely a madman—he is an outcast. His obsession with the past, his refusal to integrate into society, and his belief in the spiritual primacy of ancient tradition mark him as a relic in a modern age. Lovecraft, who often saw himself as similarly out of place, imbued the story with autobiographical longing. Kings and tombs and noble bloodlines may have been fictional, but for Lovecraft they were realer than the industrial landscape he loathed.

This modern edition aims to make "The Tomb" accessible to new readers without losing its antiquarian charm. Archaic phrases have been lightly updated, and overly dense constructions clarified, so that the story's psychological nuance and thematic richness shine through. The goal is not to modernize Lovecraft's vision, but to reveal it more clearly—to allow readers to fully inhabit the mind of Jervas Dudley as he walks that narrow path between dream and madness, memory and revelation.

Reading "The Tomb" today is to confront a question as old as humanity: What if our lives are not truly our own? What if we carry within us the dreams, fears, and destinies of those long dead? What if the tomb we fear is not just a symbol of death—but a symbol of awakening?

This edition invites you to descend into the shadows with Jervas Dudley, to explore the sealed door, the whispering wind, the candle-lit interior of a forgotten crypt. Whether you emerge believing he is mad or initiated will depend not just on the text—but on what you yourself find in the dark. For the call of the grave is not always a summons to sleep. Sometimes, it is a summons to remember. And once remembered, to never return.

The Tomb

So that I may finally rest in peace, at least in a calm and quiet place after death.

—Virgil.

As I explain the events that led to my stay in this place for the mentally ill, I understand that people might doubt my story. It's only natural—being here makes anything I say seem less believable. Sadly, most people can't think beyond what they already know. They quickly dismiss unusual things that only a few sensitive minds can see or feel, just because those things don't fit into their normal experiences. People with a deeper way of thinking understand that the line between what's real and what's not isn't always clear. The way we see the world depends on how our minds and bodies take in the world around us. But most people, focused only on what they can touch or measure, call these rare insights madness—just because they go beyond what's obvious.

My name is Jervas Dudley, and ever since I was a child, I've been a dreamer. I was born into a wealthy family, so I never had to work for a living. I also didn't fit in with the usual school life or social events like other kids did. Instead, I spent my time lost in old, rarely read books and wandering the fields and woods around my family's estate. I don't believe that what I found in those books or saw in those places was quite the same as what other children experienced—but I don't talk about that much. If I did, it would only give more reason for the quiet insults I sometimes hear whispered by the staff who watch over me. All I can do now is share what happened, without trying to explain why.

I've said that I lived apart from the world most people see—but I never said I was alone. No one can truly be alone. Without the company of others, a person starts to find connection in things that aren't alive—or things that used to be. Near my home, there was a strange wooded hollow where I spent most of my time reading, thinking, and dreaming. I took my first steps down its mossy hills as a baby, and as a child, I imagined stories around its oddly shaped oak trees. I felt like I knew the spirits of those trees and often watched them dance under the dim light of the fading moon—but I shouldn't talk about that now. I'll only speak of the old tomb hidden deep in the thickest part of the hillside forest—the forgotten tomb of the Hydes, a proud and once-powerful family whose last direct relative had been buried there long before I was born.

The tomb was made of old stone, stained and worn down by time and damp weather. Dug into the hillside, only the entrance was visible. Its heavy stone door hung slightly open, held in place by rusty iron hinges and locked with thick chains and padlocks—a creepy custom from fifty years ago. The family home had once stood above the tomb, but long ago, lightning struck during a terrible storm, and fire destroyed the mansion. Older people in the area still whisper about that storm, calling it "divine punishment," which only added to my deep curiosity about the tomb hidden in the forest. Only one person had died in the fire. The last Hyde's ashes were brought from a faraway place, where the family had gone after losing their home. No one was left to visit the tomb or lay flowers at its entrance, and most people avoided the place altogether, creeped out by the heavy shadows that clung to its weathered stones.

I'll never forget the day I first found that hidden tomb. It was a summer afternoon, the time of year when everything turns green, and the forest feels almost alive. The air was thick with the smell of wet earth and plants. In that setting, it's easy to lose track of time and feel like the past is pressing in from all sides. I had been wandering through the trees all day, thinking thoughts I can't explain and talking to things I won't name. I was only ten, but I had seen and heard things most kids hadn't—and in some ways, I felt older than my years.

While pushing my way through a patch of thorny bushes, I suddenly came face to face with the tomb's entrance. I didn't know what I had found. The dark stone blocks, the door cracked open just enough to tempt me, the carvings above the arch—they didn't seem sad or scary to me. I had read a lot about graves and tombs, but because of how I was raised, I had never actually been to a graveyard. To me, this strange stone building on the hillside was just something fascinating. I peered through the narrow opening into its cold, dark interior, but I didn't feel fear or think of death. Instead, that moment sparked something wild inside me—a deep, strange desire that eventually led me to where I am now.

It was like something in the forest itself called to me. I made up my mind to go inside, no matter what. As the daylight faded, I tried everything—shaking the chains, pushing the door, even squeezing through the small opening—but nothing worked. What started as curiosity turned into obsession. By the time I went home that evening, I had promised the ancient spirits of the forest that I would return and find a way inside that cold, silent tomb.

The doctor with the grey beard who visits my room every day once told someone that this moment was the beginning of a sad obsession. Maybe he's right. But I'll let you decide that after you've heard the whole story.

After I discovered the tomb, I spent months trying to unlock its heavy chains and padlock, but nothing worked. At the same time, I quietly started asking questions about its history. Like most curious kids, I listened carefully and learned a lot—but I never shared what I found out or what I planned to do. I wasn't scared or shocked when I learned what the tomb really was. My unusual ideas about life and death made it feel almost normal to me, like there was a strange connection between the living and the dead. I believed that the Hyde family, who had lived in the burned-down mansion, still had some presence in that dark stone chamber I wanted to enter.

Old stories about their strange rituals and wild, godless celebrations made the tomb even more fascinating to me. I would sit in front of it for hours each day. Once, I even pushed a candle through the narrow opening, but all I could see were stone steps leading down into the darkness. The smell from inside was awful—but somehow also familiar. It pulled me in. I had the odd feeling that I'd been there before, long ago, even before I was born into this body.

A year after finding the tomb, I came across an old, crumbling translation of Plutarch's Lives in the attic. When I read the story of Theseus, I was struck by the part where the young hero was meant to lift a huge stone to find his destiny. That tale changed something in me. It made me think maybe the time wasn't right yet to enter the tomb. Maybe I still needed to grow stronger or smarter before I could open the door. I told myself that when the time came, I would be ready—and until then, I should wait patiently, like fate was asking me to.

So I started visiting the tomb less often, and spent more time on other strange interests. Some nights, I would quietly sneak out to wander graveyards and burial grounds—places my parents had always kept me away from. I won't say what I did during those nights, because I'm no longer sure what was real and what wasn't. But I do remember that the next day, I'd often surprise people with strange bits of knowledge—details no one had spoken of in generations. One time, I caused a stir with a strange story about the burial of Squire Brewster, a wealthy and important man who died in 1711. His gravestone had a skull and crossbones, and was slowly falling apart. I claimed that the undertaker, Goodman Simpson, had stolen the Squire's fancy clothes before the burial—and that the Squire, not quite dead, had turned over in his coffin the next day. It sounded like a child's wild imagination, but it rattled people just the same.

Still, I never stopped thinking about the tomb. My obsession grew even deeper when I found out that, through my mother's side, I was distantly related to the Hydes. My father's family line had ended with me—and now, I realized, so had the Hydes'. That made me feel like the tomb somehow belonged to me. I began to look forward to the day I could finally enter it. I would go there at night and press my ear to the slightly open door, especially at midnight when everything was quiet. Eventually, I cleared a small space in front of the tomb, letting vines and trees grow around it so that it looked like a natural shelter. That place became sacred to me. The locked door was like an altar, and I would lie on the mossy ground, lost in strange thoughts and dreams.

The night everything changed was warm and heavy. I must have fallen asleep from exhaustion, because I remember waking up suddenly to the sound of voices. I won't describe how they sounded, only that they were unlike anything I'd ever heard. Their way of speaking was strange—some used the old language of early settlers, while others sounded like they were from a more recent time. I didn't realize this until later, though, because my attention had been pulled to something else. As I opened my eyes, I thought I saw a light flicker and then disappear inside the tomb. I wasn't sure if it really happened. I didn't panic, but something inside me changed forever. When I got home, I went straight to the attic and opened an old chest. Inside, I found a key. The next day, that key opened the tomb's chained door with ease—something I had never been able to do before.

That afternoon, with the soft light of the setting sun around me, I entered the tomb on the lonely hillside. I felt like I was under a spell. My heart pounded with a kind of joy I can't explain. I closed the door behind me and walked down the damp stone steps, holding a single candle. Even though it was dark and the air was thick with decay, I felt completely at home. All around me were marble slabs holding coffins—or what was left of them. Some were still sealed, but others had crumbled away, leaving only silver handles and small piles of pale dust. On one nameplate, I read "Sir Geoffrey Hyde," who had come from England in 1640 and died a few years later. In one shadowy alcove stood an empty coffin, still in good shape. It had a name carved into it that made me both smile and shiver. Without thinking, I climbed onto the slab, blew out the candle, and lay down inside the coffin.

At sunrise, I stumbled out of the tomb and locked the door behind me. I wasn't the same. Even though I was only twenty-one, I felt like a much older man. The early risers in the village saw me walking home and stared, confused by the signs of wild behavior on someone known for being quiet and reserved. I didn't see my parents until after I had taken a long, deep sleep.

From that point on, I returned to the tomb every night. I saw things, heard things, and did things I can never talk about. The first clear change in me showed up in the way I spoke. My voice had always been shaped by what was around me, and now it took on an old-fashioned style that people quickly noticed. Soon after, I started acting differently too. I became strangely confident and bold, even though I had spent most of my life alone. Without meaning to, I started to carry myself like someone experienced in the ways of the world.

I talked more than ever before—sometimes with the smooth charm of a gentleman, other times with the sharp sarcasm of someone who didn't care about anything. My knowledge also changed. It wasn't like the odd, dusty facts I used to read about as a boy. Now, I had a clever, polished way of writing and thinking. I scribbled witty little sayings in the blank pages of my books—phrases that reminded people of old English poets and jokers like Gay and Prior from the 1700s.

One morning at breakfast, I nearly got myself into trouble. Without thinking, I stood up and recited a rowdy drinking song from the 18th century in a voice that made me sound like I'd had a few too many myself. The strange part was that this song wasn't from any book—I had never read it. It just came to me, as if I had heard it long ago.

Come over here, my friends, and raise your mugs of ale,
Let's drink to right now before it starts to fade.
Stack your plates high with heaps of roast beef—
Because eating and drinking are the best kind of relief.
  So lift up your glass,
  Life moves by so fast;
Once you're gone, you can't toast your girl or your king in the past!

They say old Anacreon had a nose that was red,
But who cares, if you're cheerful and happy instead?
By thunder! I'd rather be red while I'm alive,
Than pale as a ghost and buried at five.
  So Betty, come here,
  Give me a kiss, dear—
There's no innkeeper's daughter like you down there!

Young Harry sits up as tall as he can,
But soon he'll drop his wig and fall like a man.
So pass round the drinks and fill them right up—
It's better to fall from a chair than rise from a cup!
  So laugh and be loud,
  Sing strong and proud—
It's harder to laugh when you're under the ground!

By the devil, I swear, I can hardly stand,
I'm stumbling and slurring and waving my hands.
Hey, barkeep—have Betty come over with a chair;
I'll head home for a bit—my wife isn't there!
  So give me some aid,
  I'm starting to fade,
But I'm happy as long as I'm still above the grave!

After that, I developed a deep fear of fire and thunderstorms. I hadn't cared about them before, but now they terrified me. Whenever a storm was coming, I'd hide in the deepest part of the house to feel safe. During the day, I often visited the burned-down ruins of the old mansion. I'd sit in the crumbling cellar and imagine what the house looked like before the fire. Once, I even surprised a local man by confidently leading him to a hidden lower cellar that had been forgotten for generations. Somehow, I just knew it was there.

Eventually, the thing I had feared the most finally happened. My parents, worried about the strange changes in my behavior, started watching me more closely. I had never told anyone about my trips to the tomb. I had protected that secret like it was sacred. But now, I had to be extra careful when sneaking through the woods. I wore the key to the tomb on a string around my neck, and no one knew it was there. I never took anything from inside the vault.

One morning, as I was leaving the tomb and locking it with a shaky hand, I saw a face peeking out from a nearby thicket—someone had been watching me. I was sure everything was about to be exposed. My hiding place had been found, and my nighttime visits to the tomb were no longer a secret. The man didn't speak to me, so I hurried home, hoping to overhear what he might tell my father. I feared he would reveal everything. But to my surprise and relief, I heard him whisper to my worried father that I had only spent the night sleeping near the tomb, my half-closed eyes fixed on the crack in the door. How he could be so wrong amazed me, and I felt like some unseen force must have been protecting me.

This gave me the confidence to stop hiding. I started visiting the tomb more openly again, trusting that no one could actually see me go inside. For a full week, I enjoyed the strange and unsettling joy I found within its walls—though I won't say exactly what I saw or did. But then, something happened that changed everything, and I was taken away to this place of sorrow and routine.

I shouldn't have gone out that night. The sky smelled of thunder, and an eerie glow was rising from the swamp at the bottom of the hill. Even the call from the tomb felt different. This time, it wasn't the vault calling me—it was the burnt cellar at the top of the hill. Something from there was drawing me in. As I walked through the trees and stepped into the open field, I saw something I'd always half expected. In the pale moonlight, the old mansion—gone for a hundred years—stood tall again, shining with the glow of hundreds of candles.

Carriages from Boston rolled up the long driveway, and groups of well-dressed people came walking from nearby estates. I joined them, even though I knew I belonged to the hosts, not the guests. Inside the mansion, there was music, laughter, and wine. I recognized some faces, but only because I imagined how they must have looked before death had taken them. Among the wild and reckless crowd, I was the most out of control. I laughed, drank, and said things that mocked every rule of man, nature, and God.

Then thunder struck—so loud it cut through the noise and stopped everyone in their tracks. Flames and choking heat rushed through the house. People screamed and ran, terrified by what felt like a punishment beyond anything natural. I stayed frozen in place, too afraid to move. And then a deeper fear took hold of me: what if I was burned to ashes, destroyed completely? I would never be laid to rest in the Hyde tomb! Wasn't that where I belonged? Didn't I have a spot waiting among my ancestors? I swore I would claim my place, even if my soul had to search for a new body to lie in that empty coffin.

As the vision of the burning house faded, I realized I was screaming and fighting in the arms of two men—one of them the same person who had followed me to the tomb. Rain poured down, and flashes of lightning lit up the sky. My father stood nearby, looking heartbroken, while I begged them to let me rest in the tomb. He kept telling the others to be gentle with me. On the ground, there was a blackened circle where the lightning had struck, and nearby, some villagers were digging up a small, old box that had been uncovered by the storm. I stopped struggling and watched them open it. Inside were papers and valuable objects—but I only cared about one thing. It was a tiny portrait of a young man with curled hair, wearing a formal wig, with the initials "J.H." on it. When I looked at his face, it felt like looking into a mirror.

The next day, they brought me here—to this room with barred windows. But I've still been able to learn a few things, thanks to an old servant named Hiram. He helped raise me and shares my love for old graveyards. He's one of the few who still believes me. What little I've said about the tomb only brings gentle smiles from others. My father visits often and insists I never actually entered the tomb. He claims the padlock hadn't been touched in fifty years. He says the whole town knew about my strange habits, and that I was often seen sleeping in the bower near the tomb with my eyes half open, staring at the crack in the door.

I can't prove him wrong. My key was lost during that awful night. Everything I learned during those visits is said to be nothing more than the result of my obsession with old books. If it weren't for Hiram, I might have believed I'd imagined everything.

But Hiram still believes. A week ago, he broke the chains on the tomb's door and went inside with a lantern. On a stone slab in one of the alcoves, he found an old but empty coffin. Its nameplate said only one word—"Jervas." They've promised me that when my time comes, I'll be buried in that tomb. In that coffin. Just like I always believed I should be.

Thank You for Reading

Dear Reader,

We hope this timeless classic has sparked your imagination and enriched your literary journey. Now that you've turned the final page, we want to share a vision for the future of reading—one where every classic you've ever wanted to explore is at your fingertips, in a format that best suits your life.

We'd like to invite you to gain immediate, unlimited digital & audiobook access to hundreds of the most treasured literary classics ever written—along with the option to secure deluxe paperback, hardcover & box set editions at printing cost. Together, we can spark a new global literary renaissance alongside our small, independent publishing house called "The Library of Alexandria."

Thousands of years ago, the Library of Alexandria stood as a beacon of knowledge—until it was lost to history. We aim to reignite that spirit of preservation and discovery right now, in the modern age—only this time, it's accessible to all, in every language and every format.

Picture a world where every timeless classic, novel, poem, or philosophical treatise is not only available to read but also updated for today's readers—modernized, translated into any language or dialect, and ready to enjoy in any format you choose, whether that is in an eBook, audiobook, paperback, or deluxe hardcover & box set version a printing cost.

By joining our movement to rebuild the modern Library of Alexandria, you become part of an unprecedented mission to offer:

- **Unlimited Audiobook & eBook Access to the Greatest Classics of All Time**

  Instantly explore thousands of legendary works, from Plato and Shakespeare to Jane Austen and Leo Tolstoy. All are instantly ready to read or listen to, giving you a complete literary universe at your fingertips.

- **Paperback & Deluxe Editions at Printing Costs:**

  Purchase any title in a paperback, deluxe hardbound, or deluxe boxset edition at printing costs, shipped right to your doorstep. Curate your personal library of Alexandria with editions worthy of display—crafted to last, designed to captivate, and delivered straight to your door.

- **Modern translations for Contemporary Readers in all languages and dialects**

  Discover a vast selection of classics reimagined in clear, current language—no more struggling with outdated phrases or obscure references. Next to the original versions, we aim to offer translations in as many languages and dialects as possible.

  As we continue our translation efforts and add new languages, readers everywhere can connect with these works as if they were written today. By bridging linguistic divides, you're contributing to ensuring that these timeless stories become more meaningful, accessible, and inspiring for people across the globe.

- **Your Personal Library of Alexandria:**

  Over the months and years, you'll curate a unique physical archive of classics—each volume a testament to your taste, curiosity, and love of knowledge. It's not just about owning books—it's about curating a cultural legacy you'll cherish and pass down for generations to come.

- **Join a Global Literary Renaissance:**

  Your support fuels an ongoing mission: allowing us to reinvest in offering deluxe print editions (including special boxsets) at their true cost, broaden the range of available formats and translations, and extend the reach of these works to new audiences worldwide. By joining today, you're not just preserving a legacy of masterpieces; you set in motion a powerful wave of literary accessibility.

We are more than a publisher—we're a movement, and we can't do it alone. Your support lets us scale our mission, preserving and reimagining history's greatest works for tomorrow's readers.

Become a Torchbearer of knowledge.

Thank you for picking up this book and allowing us into your literary journey. As you turn the pages, know that you're part of something larger: a global effort to keep these stories alive, share their wisdom across borders and generations, and spark a true cultural revival for the modern era.

If this resonates with you—please consider taking the next step by visiting:

www.libraryofalexandria.com

With gratitude and a shared love of knowledge,

The Modern Library of Alexandria Team

Visit:

www.libraryofalexandria.com

Or scan the code below:

www.ingramcontent.com/pod-product-compliance
Lightning Source LLC
Chambersburg PA
CBHW010139030826
48979CB00023B/1033

* 9 7 8 1 8 0 4 2 1 9 8 0 5 *